THIS BOOK BELONGS TO

_____

_____

_____

PUFFIN BOOKS

Published by the Penguin Group
Melbourne • London • New York • Toronto • Dublin
New Delhi • Auckland • Johannesburg • Beijing
Penguin Books Ltd, Registered Offices: 80 Strand, London WC2R 0RL, England
Published by Penguin Group (Australia), 2011
10 9 8 7 6 5
Text © Sofie Laguna, 2011
Illustrations copyright © Lucia Masciullo, 2011

Typeset in Bembo by Post Pre-press Group, Brisbane, Queensland
Printed and bound in Australia by McPherson's Printing Group, Maryborough, Victoria
National Library of Australia Cataloguing-in-Publication data available.
ISBN 978 0 14 330530 9

puffin.com.au
ouraustraliangirl.com.au

With thanks to Leanne Tobin, an Indigenous woman from the Boorooberongal clan
(Hawkesbury/Richmond area) of the Darug.

Wattle image on back cover reprinted with kind permission from the National
Gallery of Australia. **Fanny de Mole** *Gum wattle and silver wattle* 1861 from
*Wild flowers of South Australia* (Adelaide: Paul Jerrard & Son, 1861) National Gallery
of Australia, Canberra, purchased 2006.

Image on page 108 reprinted with kind permission from the National Gallery
of Australia.

*Charms on the front cover reprinted with kind permission from A&E Metal Merchants.*
*www.aemetals.com.au*

OUR
AUSTRALIAN
GIRL

# GRACE
# AND GLORY

Grace has arrived at a bark hut
at the edge of a river to start
her life as a servant. But even
though she tries hard, nothing
she does for her new master ever
seems right — especially if it
involves Glory, his beloved
horse. When her master goes
away and leaves her in charge,
will Grace know how to save her
mistress from danger?

Join Grace again on her
adventure in the third of four
exciting stories about a convict
girl who is given a second
chance.

Puffin Books

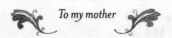 *To my mother*

OUR
AUSTRALIAN
GIRL

# GRACE AND GLORY

Sofie Laguna

*With illustrations by Lucia Masciullo*

Puffin Books

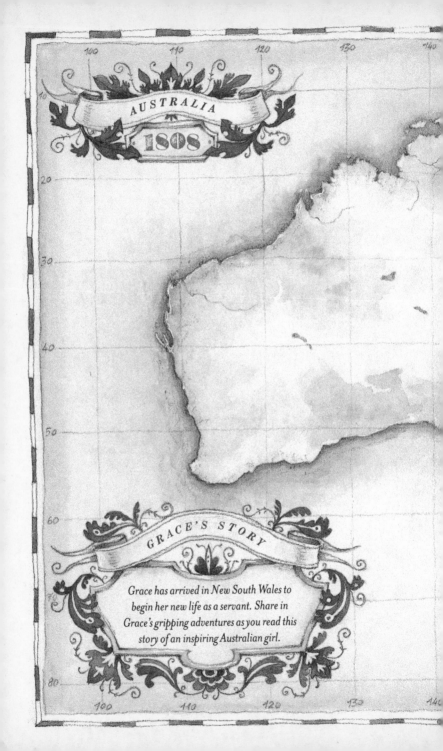

AUSTRALIA

·1808·

GRACE'S STORY

*Grace has arrived in New South Wales to
begin her new life as a servant. Share in
Grace's gripping adventures as you read this
story of an inspiring Australian girl.*

New South Wales

*Where this story takes place*

THE STORY SO FAR

As she sails up the river in Parramatta, Grace's life in London seems far behind her. Sentenced to transportation for stealing a horse, she has journeyed across the world on a convict ship and survived the Factory Above the Gaol. Now she has been chosen by Tom and Beth to be a servant. Separated from her best friend, Hannah, Grace must face the challenges of this strange land alone. Still, amid the wonders and dangers, she finds something that brings her comfort – but also heartache...

WATTLE PARK

**T**HE sun was low in the sky and the spring air growing cool when Tom, Grace's new master, rowed the small wooden boat to the river's edge. We must be close now, thought Grace, as she looked around at the cleared land sloping up from the bank.

'It's quite a walk to the property from here,' said Beth, Grace's new mistress, as she stood and rubbed her back. 'But I'll be glad to stretch my legs.'

The boat rocked and swayed in the shallows.

'Careful, my love, or we'll end up in the

water!' Tom smiled at his wife before turning to Grace. 'You get out first, and I'll pass the supplies across.'

Beth and Tom had selected Grace to be their servant from the Factory Above the Gaol in Parramatta only hours earlier. Grace had been sure they wouldn't choose her – it was clear to Grace that it wasn't Tom's idea. He wanted somebody older and stronger, but for some reason Beth had thought Grace was right for her and her husband. At the last minute, Tom had gestured to her to come out of the line of hopeful convicts and join them.

Grace was glad. She had watched Hannah and Liza, her only friends, be chosen as servants that day. The three of them had come so far together, spending five months aboard a convict ship from England before arriving at the colony and being taken to the Factory. The thought of being left behind without them was unbearable.

Now, even though Grace's heart ached with

missing them, it was a relief to be away from the Factory, with its violence and danger.

Grace clambered out of the boat, her boots sinking into the cold, muddy bottom of the river. Though the river's edge was thick with mud, Grace noticed that it didn't stink the way the shores of the Thames did back in London. It smells clean, she thought. She held out her arms for the goods Tom passed to her – a hessian sack that wriggled, a bucket filled with rope, an iron kettle, some pots and pans, and a sack of flour that she almost dropped in the water. Lastly, Grace watched as Tom carefully carried his pregnant wife from the boat to dry ground. He seems kind, thought Grace.

Grace looked at the land around her. To the far west, above the forest, she could see a range of high blue shimmering hills.

'That's the Blue Mountains you can see, Grace,' said Beth. 'Nobody can cross them 'cause they're so steep and dangerous, so nobody knows what's on the other side. Could be bloomin' fairies for all we know! And they really are blue.'

Grace thought the land looked magical. Mountains that glow blue! How she wished Hannah was here to see them, too.

Beth helped Tom strap the bundle of pots and pans to his back. Grace picked up the wriggling hessian sack along with the bucket, kettle and flour, and followed Beth and Tom up the trail leading north away from the river. Grace heard a muffled squawking coming from the sack as she walked.

'Careful with the chickens!' Tom snapped.

Grace wanted to do the right thing, and tried hard to carry the chickens without jiggling them.

On one side of the trail she saw a field neatly lined with rows of pale yellow stalks that she guessed must be some sort of crop to eat. It was Grace's first time in the country. Before coming to this new land she had spent all her life in London – a busy city. She knew about night markets and crowded rookeries and the noise of street life, but nothing about living on the land. Grace was curious about the open, quiet country around her, but also uncertain.

On the other side of the trail, the land was covered in tall brown-barked trees with long pale grass growing underneath. There aren't even any houses here! Grace thought. So far from everything, it felt as if this was a whole different world.

Just as Grace was wondering if she could take another step, Beth turned and spoke to her over her shoulder. 'We're almost there. We'll just beat the dark.'

The trail crossed a shallow creek that was narrow enough for Grace to jump without wetting her feet. Then it opened out to cleared land.

In the distance Grace saw a small cottage, uneven with a bumpy bark roof and a wooden chimney. It wasn't like the houses she knew in London, which lined up straight and were made of bricks neatly piled one on top of the other.

'Is that really going to be my new home?' Grace whispered to herself. She had never seen anything like it.

'There it is,' said Beth, stopping where she stood. '*Wattle Park*. Bloomin' lovely, isn't it? Tom and I built the house a year ago – using the same bark the natives use. Who would've thought it?'

Beth put her hands on her hips. 'The walls are tree branches plaited like a basket and then filled in with mud. I was always covered in the stuff! The trees we used are called wattles.' She pointed at the lines of shadowy trees. 'They're all around the house and they have the prettiest golden flowers you ever saw. I could've sold them on the streets of London and made a pretty penny. You are lucky you've come in spring, Grace, they will look as lovely as ever.'

Grace could tell by the way Beth was speaking that she was proud of her house.

In the fading light, Grace could make out a shed at one side of the hut, and a fence surrounding an open field. The dark moving shapes she saw in the field looked like they might be sheep, grazing.

'You go inside, Beth, before it gets much colder, and I'll take care of things out here,' said Tom. 'Grace, you help Beth.' Tom unloaded the supplies and took the sack of chickens.

'Welcome to your new home, Grace,' said Beth, pushing open the front door.

When Beth had lit three slush lamps, Grace saw that the house was made up of one room divided into two by a wall of hessian sacks hung over a wooden frame. The kitchen hearth was at one end and there were two windows, but they held no glass – only shutters made of twigs bundled together. In front of the hearth was a table that looked like it had been a wide tree growing in a forest not very long ago. On either side of the table were benches, also roughly hewn tree trunks.

'It's not fancy, but it's ours,' said Beth. 'Help me get this fire going, Grace. The spring air holds a real chill, though nothin' like the cold back home. Bet you're not sorry to leave that behind!' Beth piled sticks into the hearth and blew into them before speaking again. 'It's too late for a proper meal. Just some salted beef and bread. Tomorrow we can do better.'

'Yes, ma'am.'

When Tom came inside, the three of them ate in silence at the table, tired from their long day. Grace was so exhausted she barely tasted her food.

Beth stood and stretched. 'Grace, there's your bedding.' She pointed to a mattress rolled up in the corner of the room. 'You can wash in the morning. If I don't go to bed this minute I'll fall asleep on my feet. There are blankets and a pillow wrapped in the mattress. Should make a bed fit for a princess. Goodnight, Grace.'

'Goodnight, ma'am,' said Grace.

Beth took one of the slush lamps and disappeared behind the wall of sacks. Tom checked the fire, then followed her.

Grace lay on her back on her bed and looked up at the rough bark roof of her new home, dimly lit by the glowing embers in the fireplace. Beth coughed from the other room, and Grace listened to Tom's low whispers as he comforted her.

Grace had never had a mistress and master before. She hadn't even been a servant, and she wasn't sure that she would make a very good one with so little practice. 'How am I going to do this?' she whispered. She didn't know how to cook or work in a garden, or how to look after chickens or sheep. At least I can stoke the fire, Grace thought, and make tea for my mistress. Grace liked Beth, but Tom made her nervous.

Grace rolled onto her side and wished that her best friend, Hannah, was there. What's she doing right now? Grace wondered. Is she thinking about me? Hannah could turn every difficult thing into an adventure. Without her, Grace didn't know how she was going to make an adventure out of her new life with Beth and Tom.

Grace missed Liza, too – Hannah's mother. Liza had taken care of Grace. No one had done that since her own mother had died, which was so long ago that Grace could barely remember her. Liza had taught her what it was like to feel safe.

Grace scratched at her legs where the grass poked through her mattress. I mustn't think about Hannah and Liza, she told herself. It only makes me miss them more. I must try and be a good servant, and show Beth and Tom that they made the right choice.

Seven years – that was how long she'd have to work as a convict-servant before she'd finish her sentence. Seven years seemed like a whole lifetime away to Grace. She'd be grown up by then. She tried to picture what she'd be like, but she couldn't imagine it.

Grace listened to the quiet, gentle sounds of the forest beyond the walls of the hut – chirpings and whistling and soft rustlings. In London it was never quiet. There was always the sound of other people, everybody crowded in together – arguing and singing, laughing and shouting. The streets were noisy with the calls of the costermongers selling their wares, music men playing trumpets and drums, drunken folk pouring from the alehouses, the iron wheels of the dustman's carriage running over the cobblestones at dawn, roosters crowing, babies crying, dogs barking ...

But here the sounds were less human, and Grace lay listening to a forest lullaby made of wind and leaves and insects singing.

At last she fell asleep.

## 2

### DISCOVERIES

'Y<small>OU'D</small> best be up to light the fire and boil the water,' Tom said gruffly, stepping past Grace's bed in his trousers and undershirt.

Grace sat up with a start. She had not meant to sleep so long. She wanted to wake before first light and stoke the fire before Tom had to tell her to do it.

'Yes, sir.' Grace got out of bed and rolled up her bedding, pushing it back into the corner.

'There's water for washing at the back of the house. You'll find soap beside the pail.'

'Thank you, sir.' Grace rubbed the sleep

from her eyes. A faint light showed through the shutters covering the windows. As she crossed the room, Grace knocked over the bucket that she had carried in the day before. Tom glared at her – then pulled on his boots and left the hut. For a moment Grace was reminded of her Uncle Ord and how angry he always seemed to be with her.

She picked up the bucket shakily, stepped into her shoes and went outside, still in her smock and petticoat. She stood for a moment in the crisp, clean-smelling dawn.

Beyond the cleared land grew more of the same forest that she had seen along the river, with the trees that smelt like a mix of mint and pine. Overhead the great open sky showed the first traces of morning light. 'It's beautiful!' Grace declared. She had the same feeling she'd had when she stood on the deck of the convict ship and looked out to sea – a feeling of peace and space.

As Grace took another deep breath of fresh, clean air, she heard Beth moving around inside the house. I mustn't dawdle, she reminded herself as she walked around the back of the hut. I mustn't make a mess of my first day.

Grace washed her face and hands at the barrel and went back inside. Beth was on her knees in front of the stove trying to get the fire going by blowing into its embers.

'Let me do that, ma'am. I'll gather us some more kindling.'

'Thank you, Grace. It's like blowing on cold stones!'

Grace ran to fetch her dress, pulling it over her head as quickly as she could. She took the empty wood basket and stepped outside to search for long dry twigs that would light easily. As she filled up her basket, she heard something that held her spellbound – the long broken call of a horse. Grace's heart beat harder. A horse!

Grace loved horses. In London she had spent all her time, when she was not foraging in the mud, watching the horses at work on the busy roads or being ridden by the gentlemen round the parks. Whenever she could, she got close enough to touch them. When she was breathing in their sweet scent, everything difficult in her life disappeared. There was no struggle, and nothing to be afraid of – there was only Grace and the horse.

Grace listened for the horse to call again but she heard nothing more. As she gazed out at the land, wondering if she'd imagined the sound, she saw a tall grey animal at the forest's edge. It stood on its big hind legs, its paws in front of its chest, watching her with unblinking eyes.

Grace's skin prickled and her heart raced. It was taller than her! And it looked strong. Would it hurt her?

The animal's face was long and narrow, with pointed ears and a fine snout. A much smaller creature the same as the larger one stuck its head out of a pouch on the larger one's belly. The big one must be a mother, thought Grace, and the little one its baby! How surprising and odd they were, and how clever to carry your baby in a pouch in front! 'Perfect,' Grace said, forgetting to be afraid. I wish Hannah were here to see this, she thought. She would wish that she could be carried in a pouch!

The animal twitched its nose and then bounded into the bush, bouncing on its powerful hind legs. Grace picked up her basket and rushed back into the hut. She pushed open the front door, spilling twigs onto the floor. 'I saw an animal with a baby in its front – in a *pouch*!'

Beth turned round from the kitchen table where she had been kneading dough. Remembering her place, Grace bowed her head. 'I'm sorry, ma'am,' she said. She saw the twigs at her feet and dropped to her knees to pick them up.

Beth smiled. 'It sounds as if you've seen your first kangaroo, Grace. I like the way they carry their babies, too. We should have pouches like that! It looks ... most convenient.'

Grace looked up at her mistress. 'My first *what*, ma'am?'

'Your first *kang-ga-roo*. The name comes from the natives.'

'Is a kangaroo dangerous?' Grace asked.

'Not dangerous, though people say to stay back from the big ones because they like to box. I couldn't imagine it myself – they always run off when they see me.'

As Grace gathered up the remaining sticks and set the fire, she wondered what other strange animals she was yet to meet. She remembered the horse's call and wished she knew if there really was a horse close by.

## 3

### CORNFIELD

GRACE brought the flint down into the tinder in the stove, feeling pleased as flames crackled and the smoke rose up the chimney. 'I'll fetch the water to boil now, ma'am.'

'Make sure you watch out for the snake that lives by the water barrels,' said Beth.

'Snake, ma'am?'

'Yes. He's a big black one with a red belly. He goes away if he sees you, but he'll give you a nasty fright. I don't know what his bite would do but I know the brown ones kill you as soon as they get you. Our neighbour Mr Hill was killed by a brown only weeks ago. What a way to go!' Beth shook her head.

Grace had never seen a snake before – she had only ever thought about them as magical creatures from stories, the kind Hannah liked to tell her to make her squeal. 'But, ma'am, what do I do if I see him?'

'I just bang a stick against the barrels and shout for him to go away. And mind you never go out there without your shoes on. There's spiders what live in holes in the grass and if they bite the bottom of your foot, you're gone faster than if the brown snake bit you!'

Snakes and spiders that kill you? Kangaroos that like to box and carry babies in their pouches? Houses made of branches and mud? What a place! How will I survive even one day? Grace thought. And yet, at the same time as being scared, she felt excited.

Grace picked up the water bucket and

carried it around to the barrels.'Go away, snake!'
she called. 'I would like to see your magic
red belly so that I could tell Hannah about
it, but not today. *Not today!*' When the snake
made no appearance, Grace was both relieved
and disappointed. As she filled the bucket she
noticed how thick the forest grew where it had
not been cleared. Grace had never known that
the world could hold such a forest of smoke-
coloured trees with such twisted branches. She
could stand and look at it for days.

She lugged the heavy bucket of water back
inside the house. It spilled over the sides and
wet her dress and the sacks covering the floor.
'Here, ma'am, sorry, ma'am,' she said to Beth,
who stood grinding leaves with a pestle and
mortar.

'Thank you, Grace.'

Grace was glad when Beth didn't seem
to mind about the spilled water. 'What next,
ma'am?'

Beth looked uncomfortable. 'Tom has something he wanted you to do – but ...'

'Yes, ma'am?'

'It's not an easy chore for your first day ... He wants you to keep the crows and parrots from eating our corn. We planted Indian corn for the animals and it's coming up nice and yellow. The parrots will already be at it.' Beth chewed at her lip. 'It's a long day out there, what with nobody to talk to and a job better suited to a scarecrow.'

'I don't mind, ma'am.'

'It will only be for a little while longer, and then the crop will be ready for harvesting and we won't have to worry about it another day.'

'I'll look after the corn, ma'am.'

'Oh, that's brave of you, Grace. The cornfield is behind the house and down toward the creek. Just follow the little trail that starts at the water barrels – you can't miss it. You have to run at the birds and scream at them, they get so bold.'

'Yes, ma'am.'

'When you see the sun going down behind the hill, it's time to come home. Find yourself a nice big stick on the way and make sure you swish it through the grass ahead of you to scare off them snakes.'

Grace swallowed. 'Yes, ma'am.'

'And Grace.' Beth pressed her lips together. 'Sometimes the natives come to the property. I give flour and sugar to one in particular. Her name is Mulgo. She has shown me some good herbs to gather from the bush. Her children are very curious – they might stand and gawk at you but they won't give you any trouble.'

'What do they look like?' Grace asked, intrigued.

'They look ... different. They don't wear clothes for one thing – maybe furs over their shoulders, but that's it – and the men carry spears. But don't be scared, Grace. Just watch over the corn and leave them be.'

'Yes, ma'am.' The way Beth talked about the natives didn't make them sound so dangerous – not like the brown snakes and the spiders in holes. And one of them had a name – Mulgo.

'Before you go, I'll make some porridge for our breakfast. If you see it moving in your bowl, don't worry – it's just the weevils. Sometimes they're the only meat Tom and I eat!'

'I'm used to weevils, ma'am,' Grace said. 'I ate enough of them on the ship coming over.' Beth's smile reminded her of the way a flower opens, and Grace couldn't help but smile back.

But as she ate her breakfast, Grace wasn't sure how she should speak with her mistress. She felt shy and worried that she might say the wrong thing, and that Beth would soon learn how little she knew about being a servant.

Beth's next words broke the silence. It was as if she knew what Grace was thinking. 'You know, Grace, when I first came to this country all I knew were the streets of London. But you learn as you go.' She smiled at Grace again and it made her feel less unsure of herself, and less alone.

Beth put down her spoon and looked at Grace. 'Was it very hard for you to leave England? Did you have to leave your mother behind?'

Grace hesitated. The only person she had told about her life in London was Hannah. Not even Liza knew about Uncle Ord and why she had run away.

'Oh Grace, excuse my nosey questions – I haven't had someone to talk to in so long. Tom's out working much of the time, and I'm mostly alone. Sometimes I think it'll send me raving mad.' Beth stood, gathering up the dirty bowls.

Grace took a deep breath. 'I didn't have to leave my mother. I don't know my mother, ma'am. I only left my uncle, and that was before I was sent to prison.'

Beth sat back down. 'I'm sorry to hear that, Grace.'

The way Beth looked at her, so soft and sad, made Grace want to tell Beth about Hannah and Liza and how much she missed them, how much it hurt to leave them. But she feared that if she did, Beth might think she was weak and wouldn't make a good servant. She swallowed hard. 'It doesn't matter ma'am.' Grace paused. 'I am glad I'm here.'

Beth placed her hand over Grace's. 'I'm glad, too.' Beth's hand felt warm and steady, and Grace meant what she had said. She was glad.

Before Grace left the house, Beth gave her some hard bread, a small piece of salted beef wrapped in cloth and a bottle half-filled with water. 'For your lunch, Grace.'

'Thank you, ma'am.'

'Tom will be happy you kept the birds from the corn.'

'Yes, ma'am,' said Grace. She would keep the birds away all night, too, if it would make her new master happy.

# 4
## GLORY

GRACE followed the trail that led to the cornfield, past trees thick with fluffy golden flowers. They must be those wattle trees Beth spoke about last night, Grace thought as she walked. How pretty! She heard clucking and squawking. And they must be the chickens I carried from the boat. They sound much happier today!

The trail passed through a field where Grace saw a small herd of sheep grazing on the cleared land surrounded by forest. Not so long ago it would *all* have been forest, Grace thought.

Beth and Tom have been working hard.

At the bottom of the hill, Grace came to a field planted with rows of corn stalks that were a much brighter green than the leaves all around. The corn was taller than Grace.

A lone tree stood close to the field. That shall be my guarding place, Grace decided. On the way to the tree, she searched through the grass for a long stick, expecting to see a snake jump out at her at any minute. Once she found the right stick, long and pointed, she stood by her tree and waited. Sure enough, soon black crows began to fly over the corn. Grace ran at them screaming. The crows flew up into the air, then dived back down into the corn. Grace imagined that the birds were Joe Bean and his gang – the mudlarks who used to bully her back in England. She ran at them with her stick raised high. 'Get away you devil birds! Get away!' she shouted.

Then came a cloud of bright red parrots.

They were so striking and bold that Grace
wanted to stand and just watch them. But they
attacked the corn, too, with their hooked beaks,
and she ran at them as hard as she could. 'Leave
Beth's corn alone! Get away!' she shouted.

After Grace had been at her guarding place
an hour or more, the land seemed to go still
and quiet. Clouds hung motionless in the
enormous sky, the trees stopped whispering to
each other in the wind; even the birds were
silent. Grace had never seen the world so quiet
and so alive at the time. She felt as if she were
being watched by the land itself and the feeling
unnerved her.

If Hannah were here, we could chase each
other in and out of the corn – that would keep
the birds away, she thought. How Grace missed
laughing with her friend.

Suddenly, she heard the same call she had
heard earlier that morning – 'Neigh-eigh-
eigh!' A horse – and it was close by! 'I wasn't

dreaming!' Grace said. She wished desperately that she could go and see the horse for herself. But what if the birds eat the corn while I'm gone? she worried. Tom would be angry.

At that moment the horse called again, 'Neigh-eigh-eigh!' It was as if it knew Grace was there and was tempting her to come. Perhaps if I'm only gone for a minute, she thought, just to see for myself if it really is a horse, and then rush back, it will be as if I never left . . .

Grace dropped her stick and ran up the hill. When she looked down the other side, she saw a tall shining bay mare, with a sleek black mane, hobbled and feeding on the grass.

Grace's heart was pounding. When she got close, she held out her hand. The horse lifted her fine head and looked at Grace with large dark eyes. As Grace stepped closer, the horse blew a snort of breath from her nostrils and shook her head. When Grace was near enough to touch her, she sniffed Grace's hair, and Grace put her arms around the horse's high, strong shoulders.

The horse's smell reminded her of Pegasus, the horse she had loved back in London – the horse the gypsy had told her was her very own. Grace breathed in the mare's scent more deeply, and all of the hard things in her life disappeared. There was no master and mistress to disappoint, no best friend to long for, no Liza to need, no deadly snakes or hungry crows. There was only Grace and the horse.

'What you think you're doing? Hey!'

Grace lifted her head to see her master striding towards her, and gasped.

'Why aren't you looking over the corn? What do you think you're doing coming so close to Glory?' Tom was flushed and breathing fast.

'Oh, sir, oh sir, I – I . . .' Grace felt blood rush to her face.

Tom stood by his mare. 'This is not what we brought you here for. You're a servant – you are working for us, not free to roam as you were on the streets.'

Grace felt her cheeks burn. She was terrified that his next words would be 'It's time we sent you back to the Factory.'

'Yes, sir, I'm very sorry, I didn't – I didn't . . . '

'And you're to call me *Master Tom*.'

'Yes, sir, of course, sir, I mean, yes Master . . . Master Tom,' Grace stammered.

'Back to the field!'

Grace fled. As she returned to the cornfield, she saw flocks of the red birds with the blue wings diving in and out of the corn. 'Get away from there, get away, get away!' she shouted at the birds, as loud and angry as Tom had been with her.

When she reached her tree, Grace burst into tears. She didn't take her eyes from the corn for the rest of the day. Even when her eyes burned from the strain and the sun, and her head ached, Grace did not look away.

GRACE waited until it was almost dark before leaving the field to follow the track back up to the hut. She felt tired. Her back ached from standing so long, and the skin on her nose and cheeks stung.

How will I ever be anything but *dispensable*? she thought as she walked, her head down. A good servant doesn't run away from her work to go and touch somebody else's precious horse.

Grace wondered if Tom knew about Pegasus. No wonder he was worried about having me around his horse, and no wonder he never wanted me here, she thought. He thinks I'm a thief. He wouldn't know that I only wanted to give Pegasus apples to keep him going and that I didn't mean any harm.

Even though Grace knew she wasn't a thief, Tom made her feel guilty and ashamed of herself – so different to the way she had felt when she was with Liza. Hannah's mother was proud of her, and told her she was clever, brave and helpful. Grace wished they'd never had to be separated. She longed for Hannah, too. Why did I meet a best friend if I was only going to lose her again? she wondered.

Grace was so caught up in her worries that she didn't notice Beth coming towards her with a small lamp that glowed and bounced as she walked.

'Grace,' she called. 'I thought I was going to have to come down to the corn and find you! I was scared those awful birds had carried you away!'

As Beth drew closer, the soft light of the lamp showed Grace the concern in her mistress's eyes. She thinks that she hasn't picked a good servant after all, Grace thought. She was sure that Tom must have told Beth what she had done that day – how she had left the field to go and see his horse.

But Beth touched her shoulder lightly. 'You must be very hungry,' she said. 'It's hard work, I know. Only those flamin' parrots for company. I'm in the middle of cooking us all a good supper to make up for last night.'

Tom can't have told her what happened, Grace thought, relieved – she is so kind. Beth and Grace walked up the trail together, the lamp casting a soft light ahead of them.

When they entered the hut, Grace saw Tom sitting by the hearth rubbing oil into Glory's saddle. Beth went to him and kissed his shoulder, and he smiled up at her. Grace swallowed, her throat dry. But Tom did not say anything to his wife and he didn't acknowledge Grace at all.

Grace watched Beth turn the meat that was roasting over the fire and avoided Tom.

'You'll taste your first kangaroo tonight,' Beth said, not noticing Grace's nerves. 'Tom went hunting. It isn't like the meat from home, but with enough pumpkin on your fork you won't taste the difference.'

'We are eating the kangaroo?' Grace asked.

'It's that or go hungry. The pumpkin will help it down. They grow more easily here than other things.'

Grace watched as Beth sprinkled pepper over the meat.

'The pepperberry grows wild in the bush,' Beth said. 'Mulgo showed me. You grind the dried berries and end up with pepper. Saves me having to buy it in town from the supplies shop. Grace, can you lift the lid off the stove and tell me if you think the vegetables are ready?

Make sure you use the cloth or you'll burn your fingers.'

Grace lifted the heavy iron lid from the stove and placed it on the stone at the foot of the hearth. 'What shall I do now, ma'am?' She wished she didn't have to ask. She wished she knew how to cook dinner, but she hadn't a clue.

'You can call me Beth, for a start. Whenever you say "ma'am" I expect my old mistress to turn up in the kitchen and make life a misery for all of us!' Beth smiled as she stoked the fire.

'Yes . . . Beth.' Grace stole a look at Tom, who was polishing his boots. *Master Tom* and *Beth* . . . I mustn't forget.

'Stick the knife into the pumpkin and if it slides in easy as butter, it's ready to eat. And you can check the onions have browned just by looking at them.'

Grace did as she was told. The knife sunk easily into the pumpkin and the onions were golden brown and crisped at the edges. 'I think they're ready, Beth.'

'Good timing,' said Beth, lifting the meat from the fire. 'Now fetch us some plates from the shelf and bring them to the table.'

Grace saw a stack of four plates on the shelf. How many shall I take down? she wondered. Am I to eat with my mistress and master, or after them? Grace decided it was safest to just take down two plates.

'Set them at the table, please, Grace. It's our finest china, never mind the chips.' Beth laughed.

'What about the spoons, ma'am?' Grace asked. 'I mean – Beth.'

'The cutlery's in the wooden box – knives and forks for tonight's banquet, Grace.'

Grace took two forks and two knives from the box and set them beside the plates. She wasn't used to being allowed to use a knife and fork. In the Factory and on the boat, the prisoners had only been given spoons. Now she felt foolish for not knowing better. Does the cutlery need to sit above the plates? she wondered. Or across them? When she had played toffs and princesses with Hannah, they had pretended their wooden spoons were shiny silver ones but they had never talked about how to set a table. Grace wished very much that they had. The last thing she wanted to do was make another mistake.

'Grace, you've only put out two plates.' Beth turned from the kitchen bench and came to the table. Grace looked at the floor. 'Aren't you hungry after your day at the cornfield?'

As if her stomach was answering Beth's question, it growled loudly. Grace flushed and kept her eyes on the floor.

'Take down another plate, Grace. This hut is too small for you to go to a different room while we eat. You can't very well go outside. It wouldn't be right.' Beth pointed to the place at the other side of the head. 'You can put it there.'

Grace almost wished she could eat separately,

the way servants in England did. Liza had
worked for a fancy mistress in London and
she had told the girls that servants always ate
separately and only got the scraps. As Grace took
down another plate, she wondered if she would
ever understand how things were to work here.

'Grace, the pumpkin can go in the blue
dish – yes, that's the one. Tom, dinner!'

Beth winked at Tom as he sat down.
'Just pretend the stinging nettles are English
spinach, my love,' she said as she ladled green
leaves onto each plate.

'As long as the leaves don't sting my tongue,
I'm happy to pretend it's anything at all.' Tom
smiled at his wife.

Grace could see from the light in his eyes how
much he loved her. They are a family – they
belong together. I can never imagine having
fun with Tom, she thought as she sat down. He
just seems disappointed or cross with me.

Beth stretched out her hands towards Grace

on her left and her husband on her right. Tom also extended a hand to Grace.

'It's time to give thanks to God, Grace,' Beth said, taking Grace's hand firmly in her own. Grace felt the pressure of Tom's warm hand on one side and Beth's on the other. We make a circle, she thought, and closed her eyes.

As she ate, Grace did not look away from her kangaroo, which she was enjoying far more than she expected; the meat tasted sweet and peppery at the same time.

Tom spoke to his wife between mouthfuls. 'Jerry told me some new folk have moved into Mr Hill's property. A man called William Clay – he's a free settler from Hampshire. He's brought his new wife with him, too. She could make a friend for you in time. Jerry said she's very capable. I think she has some sort of experience with helping the sick.'

Jerry must be a neighbour, Grace thought, or a friend of Tom's.

'The road to the property isn't cleared yet, though – the East Trail that runs down by the creek,' Tom continued. 'But it will be soon and then Jerry could take you in the wagon – it'd take about an hour. I know how lonely it gets when I am away.'

'Oh! That's good news. My only friend has been Mulgo, and we barely understand a word each other says! Pair of right fools we look, trying to have a conversation.' Beth smiled, then looked at Grace. 'But I won't be so lonely now that I have some help.'

Grace lifted her face and her mistress's clear blue eyes drew a smile from her.

'You mustn't call Mulgo your friend, Beth.' Tom frowned at his wife. 'She's a native! They aren't to be trusted.'

'But Tom, Mulgo has only ever helped me –' Beth protested.

Grace had heard a lot of different things about the natives since she'd arrived at the colony, and she wondered which ones were true.

'She hasn't given us any trouble,' Tom continued, 'but you know very well there are settlers who've lost livestock and property to those savages! They're uncivilised and you're to steer clear.'

Beth pulled back from her husband. 'But Mulgo gave me medicine when I was so sick, back when I was first pregnant, don't you remember?'

'And she was given sugar and flour for her troubles. She's a savage, Beth, just like the rest of them. I don't wish them any harm, like some of the settlers do, but we should leave them alone.' Tom drank from his cup. 'In a few days I'll have to go away,' he said.

Beth sighed. 'In a few days? Tom, so soon?'

'Better now than in a few more weeks when the baby will be very close.' Tom placed his hand against his wife's round belly.

'Yes, I suppose that's true ... though I wish you didn't have to go at all.'

'I know, but Jerry and I stand to make good money helping a team to clear some land at the foot of the mountains. And when I return there will be enough for another cow.'

'Another cow? What about a fine dress for me to wear while I milk the one we've already got?' Beth's eyes danced.

Tom laughed. 'How about a cow *and* a fine dress to go with it!'

The way Beth and Tom teased and played reminded Grace of Hannah and the fun they used to have. Her chest was filled with longing.

The feeling lasted into the evening. Grace lay in her bed, thinking about the kindness in Glory's eyes. As she drifted into sleep, she imagined that she, too, had a horse of her own. She imagined looking deep into its eyes and breathing in its scent and riding far away from this world where she never seemed to belong.

## 6
### WORK

FOR the rest of her first week at Wattle Park, Grace watched over the corn. One morning, as she was passing the storage shed on her way to the field, she saw Tom preparing Glory for a ride. Grace stopped and stood quietly as he slipped a bridle over his horse's head. She noticed how he pressed the silver bit against Glory's lips so that she opened her mouth for him and he could slide in the silver bar. She watched him buckle the strap against Glory's cheek, speaking softly to her as he worked. 'I'm going to take you for a ride, Glory girl. We'll go as fast as the wind today – even faster ...'

He's so gentle with her, thought Grace, sighing.

At that moment, Tom looked across and saw Grace leaning against the shed watching him. 'Get down to that cornfield, Grace!'

'Yes, sir – sorry, sir,' Grace stammered.

Just as she turned away, she saw something move across the ground towards Glory. Grace narrowed her eyes and peered into the grass. The thing emerged between the long tufts. It was a snake! A brown snake! The kind that could kill you with a single bite. As the snake's long and powerful body slithered through the grass towards Glory, Grace was filled with horror.

She screamed.

The mare pulled back in fright, yanking the reins from Tom's hands and knocking him off balance.

'A snake!' Grace cried. 'A snake!'

Tom grabbed hold of Glory's reins to stop the horse from backing away.

Grace pointed to the grass at Glory's feet, her arm shaking. 'Oh, sir, there's a snake! A snake is coming for your horse, sir!'

'Where? Where did you see it?' Tom spun around, searching through the grass.

Grace pointed. 'There, sir, there!'

Tom kicked at the ground with his boots. 'Are you sure it was a snake?'

'Yes, sir. A brown one! The kind that can kill you!'

Tom picked up a long stick from the ground and swung it through the grass.

'Be careful!' Grace's panicked voice frightened Glory again, and the horse reared away from her master.

But Tom couldn't find the snake. He dropped the stick and looked darkly at Grace. 'There's no snake here. And keep your voice down. You're upsetting the horse.'

But Grace knew what she had seen. 'There was a snake, sir. I saw it with my own eyes! You must lead Glory away!'

Tom stroked his horse's neck. 'Hush girl, hush there . . . ' He turned back to Grace. 'Get down to the cornfield. You're supposed to be watching over my corn, not standing around telling me what to do with my horse!'

Grace knew she shouldn't have been watching Tom. But she knew, too, that if she hadn't called out, the snake would still have been slithering towards Glory. Maybe it would have bitten her.

Grace was still shaking from the fright the snake had given her and the words burst out of her. 'I know what I saw, sir. It was a snake and it was coming for Glory!'

'I told you to mind your business and get to the cornfield!' Tom snapped. 'There's no blasted snake here!'

Grace suspected she was not a very good servant, but she knew she was no liar. She turned towards the trail, her heart pounding and her legs shaking. 'I saw it with my own eyes,' she whispered to herself. The ground spun beneath her feet. When she looked down it seemed very far away. She couldn't believe that she had spoken to her master like that. But it had been right to call out and warn him about the snake. Grace took a deep breath and kept walking.

At the end of the week it was time to harvest the corn, but Grace wasn't tall enough to reach the husks with the husking peg. For the first day Beth helped her husband but he soon sent her back up to the hut.

'He thinks I'm too pregnant,' she said to Grace. 'Well, he can do it himself and I'll show you how to work the garden, since the corn won't need minding. You must be pleased about that, Grace,' she said, grinning.

Beth took Grace to the vegetable patch. She

had planted turnips, radishes, onions, pumpkins and cabbages in neat rows on a large square of turned earth.

'It'll be your job to pull out all these weeds, and pick off these bloomin' sticky slugs and snails – oh, and water everything,' she told Grace, plucking at a beetle as it crawled across a leaf on a pumpkin vine.

'Where did you learn to make a vegetable garden, Beth?' Grace asked as they pulled up fat white and pink turnips from the dark soil. 'Is that what you did in England?' Grace had noticed that Beth didn't mind mentioning the past, but Tom never mentioned it at all.

'Blimey, no!' she said. 'I used to sell chestnuts and watercress and violets and anything else I could get at a good price. That is, until I couldn't afford market price and I stole myself some fine lace to sell. That's how I ended up here.'

It was easy for Grace to imagine being on the convict ship with Beth, or buying roast chestnuts from her on the streets of London. Grace already felt as if she had known Beth a long time, even though it hadn't been long at all.

'But if I hadn't learned how to garden,' Beth continued, 'we'd have nothing to eat out here but bloomin' kangaroo. I talk to a couple of the other wives when I go into town, and Jerry has shown me a few things. Plenty of convicts and settlers go hungry just because they don't want to get their hands dirty or eat anything that they didn't eat back in England. All they want is beef and mutton. But I'll try anything – and so will Tom. He taught himself to catch fish by watching the other coves on the river.'

As Grace looked down, she was caught by surprise. A fat white grub was wriggling across her hand. 'Aaahhhhh!' she shrieked.

Beth laughed. 'I'll bet that grub would taste good with a bit of sugar and butter! Why don't you give it a try, Grace?'

'Uch!' Grace laughed too. 'No, thank you!'

'Oh, go on, what's wrong with you?' Beth picked the wriggling worm off Grace's wrist and dangled it over her own mouth.

'Beth, no!' Grace giggled, trying to grab it from Beth's hand.

Beth opened her hands wide to show there was no worm. 'As if I would! What do you take me for?'

Grace curtsied. 'A lady, just like me!'

Sometimes when Beth joked around, she reminded Grace of a wild girl, and not a mistress and a landowner and a mother-to-be. It made Grace like her even more.

'And you are quite the lady – a very pretty one at that. Have you seen yourself lately?' Beth took Grace's hand. 'Come with me.'

Grace followed her mistress into the hut. Beth went behind the partition and returned to the kitchen with a small mirror.

'Now take a look at yourself, my lady!' Beth handed the mirror to Grace. 'You have grown quite bonny since you arrived. When I first saw you, what a pale, thin thing you were, with no colour in your cheeks and no meat on your bones.'

Grace took the mirror from Beth and looked at her reflection. She hardly recognised herself. Her skin had turned a golden brown and there was a fine peppering of freckles across her nose. Her eyes shone back at her brightly, and though her hair could have been neater, it too looked shiny.

'I look – I look *well*!' Grace blurted.

'You do indeed,' Beth smiled. 'It's all that kangaroo, sunshine and hard work. Now, my fine lady, let us take to the garden and dig us up some snails for our dinner!' Grace laughed and her sunny new reflection laughed with her.

That night, Grace, Beth and Tom ate their evening meal together for the last time before Tom left for the week. As soon as he sat down, he turned to Grace. 'I want you to do all the heavier chores while I'm away,' he said. 'I've cut a pile of wood for the fire – make sure the house always has enough so that Beth won't have to carry it inside.'

'Yes, sir. I mean, yes M–'

'Tom!' Beth cut in. 'I'm not a bloomin' invalid. I'm just having a baby!' She tugged playfully on her husband's shirtsleeve.

'But you only have a few weeks to go and I want you to take care of yourself. When your time is nearer I'll bring Olive Diggs from town to deliver the baby. I've heard she's the best midwife in Parramatta.' Tom turned back to Grace. 'Carry the water up from the creek while I'm gone, and milk Moll. Is that clear?'

'You think I'll break the milking stool 'cause I've gotten so fat!' Beth teased.

'I'm serious, Beth. I don't want to worry while I'm away.'

'Of course, Tom. But there's no need – I'll

do nothing but put my feet up the whole time you're gone.'

'Good!' Tom smiled.

'And *I* don't want to worry while you're away with Jerry,' said Beth. 'Don't stand under any trees when they're falling, and watch Jerry doesn't drink too much whiskey when he's driving the wagon!'

'Yes, my dear. Jerry and I will return safe and sound next Sunday.'

'I'll look forward to it. But that's enough talk of our time apart. Tonight I've made something special for your dessert from those big pink Rosella flowers that you see growing in the bush. Mulgo showed them to me.'

Grace cleared the bowls while Beth drew hot damper from the coals. She cut three slices of the crusty bread and placed one in each bowl. Grace took the small enamel jug from the kitchen bench and brought it to the table. She enjoyed helping Beth serve the supper; it made her feel useful. Each day she was growing more used to working with her mistress. And Grace had noticed other changes in herself. She felt stronger – it didn't tire her to carry heavy firewood or loads of wet washing up the hill from the creek. She could walk for miles, without her legs feeling sore or weak. When she looked down at her arms, they looked stronger, too, and her skin had turned the colour of golden toffee.

'You can do the pouring, Grace,' said Beth.

Grace poured the sweet pink syrup over the steaming damper. She glanced at Beth in admiration, and noticed that Tom was doing the same.

THE next morning, as Grace left the house to bring in more wood, she saw a man riding a small horse-drawn wagon towards the property. She rushed back inside. 'Master Tom, I think your neighbour is here to collect you.'

He nodded at her from where he sat at the kitchen table, swallowing the last of his tea. He picked up his hunting rifle and canvas bag of supplies, and went outside.

Beth came out from behind the hessian curtain, still in her nightdress. 'Grace, can you fetch some damper for the men?'

Grace took the loaf outside where Tom was loading his gear onto the wagon. A man with a thick red beard came out from the other side and adjusted the leathers on the grey horse.

'Grace, this is Jerry.'

Grace bowed her head. 'Yes, sir – yes, Master Tom.' *Why do I always forget how to speak when I'm around him?* Grace blushed.

'Good morning, Grace.' Jerry smiled warmly at her. 'Feeling a long way from home out here?'

'Yes, sir.'

'We all do at first.' Jerry climbed up onto the wagon.

Tom secured his things on the tray before speaking to Grace. 'You're to leave Glory alone while I'm gone, Grace. Do you understand?'

'Yes, Master Tom.' Grace felt herself blush all over again.

'You ready, *Master Tom*?' Jerry grinned and

pulled his wide-brimmed hat low on his head, picking up the reins. His grey horse pulled at the bit. How I wish I could feed the horse some turnip before he goes! Grace thought.

Beth came out of the hut wearing her work dress. 'Hello, Jerry!'

'Morning, Beth.' Jerry lifted his hat as he greeted Beth.

'Take care of my husband while you're gone, Jerry, and I'll reward with you with the finest supper in the land when you return.'

'I'll hold you to that, Beth!' Jerry grinned, jamming his hat back down onto his head.

Grace watched as his horse pulled at the reins, eager to begin the journey. I wish I had my own horse and a wagon for my things, Grace thought, envying Jerry.

'Goodbye, Tom!' Beth embraced her husband. 'Take care, my love.' They held each other for a long moment before parting. Beth wiped her eyes with the back of her hand.

'Go on you two, get going before we need to serve you supper!'

Jerry clicked his tongue and tapped the reins against the grey's dappled back. 'Get up there, Billyboy!'

Grace stood beside her mistress and watched Billyboy pulling the men away in the wagon. When they had disappeared over the hill she followed Beth inside.

'Time for some spring-cleaning, Grace. Let's turn our little home inside out,' said Beth, tying her apron around her stomach.

'But you know you're not to work too hard,' said Grace, taking the apron Beth offered her.

'Oh, don't you listen to Tom.' She put a hand on her belly. 'The baby is still a long way off. We'll start with the floors and work our way up.'

Grace felt uneasy – she knew that things could go wrong with babies. She remembered the night her neighbour in London, Ma Honeywell, had nearly died having a baby that had got stuck inside her. One of her other daughters had to race across town and fetch the midwife to help the baby out. And Ma Honeywell was used to having babies – how many did she have? Eleven? Grace had lost count. Remembering Ma Honeywell's screaming that night made Grace feel nervous.

But Beth was her usual energetic self. She and Grace gathered up the sacks that covered the hut's dirt floor, took them outside, hung them over the fence railing and beat them until the dust rose up in clouds. Beth sang as she worked and Grace hummed along with her cheerful tune. Though the work was hard, the spring sun was shining, warming her body, and she felt light and happy. Tom is gone for a week! Grace thought. A whole week.

As she was following Beth inside, carrying the clean sacks, she saw a dark-skinned woman standing by a tree near the fence. Her heart raced. One of the natives, she thought. A child clung to the woman's legs.

'Beth, Beth!' Grace called.

'What is it, Grace?'

'I think you had better come back outside.'

Beth stuck her head out the door. 'What is it?'

Grace nodded in the direction of the woman by the tree.

'Ah, Mulgo!' Beth waved, before going back inside. She came out a moment later with a small cloth bag. 'Come with me, Grace.'

Grace followed her mistress towards the woman. She felt shy looking at someone with so few clothes on, but Beth didn't seem bothered at all.

The only thing Mulgo was wearing was a cloak over her shoulders that looked like it was made of squares of possum fur. Grace had seen possums running along the fence when she had gone out at night. On Mulgo's chest and on the tops of her arms Grace noticed a pattern of tiny marks that looked like scars. The pattern reminded Grace of ripples on water and she could see that the marks had been put there on purpose, as if they had a special meaning. Over her shoulder Mulgo carried a string bag.

As they drew closer, the little boy hid behind Mulgo and peeked out at Grace. He giggled, his dark eyes watchful and mischievous. Grace saw that the woman held a bunch of red and orange flowers that looked like round red hairbrushes.

'Mulgo!' said Beth, holding out the cloth bag. 'Some sugar for you!'

Mulgo smiled back and Grace noticed how white the woman's teeth were against her dark skin. Her legs and arms and back all look strong, thought Grace. And she wouldn't grow pink in the sun like Beth and I do.

Mulgo's little boy held onto his mother's leg. He looked at Grace and grinned, his eyes bright, his cheeks as plump and smooth as dark plums.

'More sugar.' Beth shook the bag.

The native woman's eyes flickered over Grace.

'Mulgo – this is Grace,' Beth said. '*Grace*. She's your friend too.' Beth put her arm around Grace.

Mulgo looked at Grace for a long moment before taking the bag of sugar. She then turned to Beth and held out the brush-like flowers.

'What have you got there?' asked Beth.

'*Bool*,' Mulgo said, nodding towards the tree.

Beth stepped closer. Mulgo pointed to a knobbly bowl shape in the trunk of the tree. It was filled with water and two of the brush flowers floated in it. Grace wondered why the flowers were sitting in water.

Mulgo cupped her hand and, using it as a ladle, she dipped it into the bowl in the tree. '*Bool*, Beddi,' she said, before bringing her hand to her mouth and drinking. '*Bool*,' she said again.

'Come on, Grace,' said Beth. 'She wants us to do the same.'

Beth and Grace stood beside Mulgo and dipped their hands into the tree's bowl. How clever, thought Grace. No need for washing up! She cupped her hands and drank. The cool liquid surprised her – it was as sweet as honey. She wiped her hand across her mouth. 'Delicious,' she said.

'It's the nectar from the flowers, Grace,' said Beth, dipping in her hand for another drink. 'Even better than the lemonade sold on Clare Street!'

Mulgo looked at Beth, smiling, and held out the flowers.

'Take them, Grace,' said Beth.

Grace took the prickly flowers from Mulgo as Beth gave Mulgo the sugar and Mulgo's little boy chased a butterfly across the garden.

'Beddi,' said Mulgo, raising her hand before walking away.

Grace looked at Beth. 'Beddi?' she said. 'Is that what she calls you? I like that.'

'To you I am Beth!' Beth laughed. 'Let's take these inside.'

Grace watched as Mulgo walked away. She wondered what it would feel like to carry a special meaning in the marks on your skin, and to cross the ground in bare feet, and to not feel the stones or the prickling grasses. She mustn't even be afraid of snakes, Grace thought. Tom spoke about the natives as though they couldn't be trusted, but Grace was only curious.

Back inside the house, Beth placed some of the flowers in a jar of water and arranged them on the kitchen table. In the shaded light of the hut, the red and orange brush flowers looked warm and bright.

Beth put the remaining blossoms in a shallow tub of water. 'This afternoon we'll drink our own bool, Grace. As a reward for our hard work. Now let's go wash some clothes.'

'Yes, Beddi!' said Grace.

'*Beth*, if you please!' laughed her mistress.

## 8

## PAIN

As Beth and Grace carried the dirty clothes down to the creek in baskets, Beth spoke about the natives. 'Some of the settlers have real trouble with them stealing corn and the like – there have been some awful shootings. It don't seem right to me, when they have only spears and we have guns. I don't see why we can't all get along and even learn a few things from each other.' Beth shifted her basket of clothes to her other hip. 'That's not how Tom feels, though. He thinks the same as most of the other settlers and he doesn't want me to have anything to do with Mulgo, even though she gave me that wonderful bush medicine. She shows me how to use the leaves and berries that grow around here, too. She can turn bloomin' stinging nettles into spinach! If that's not clever I don't know what is!'

Grace didn't like to think about the natives being shot; she hoped Mulgo and her son would always be safe.

When they reached the creek, Grace copied Beth, taking off her boots and stockings and sitting on the stones that lined the bank. She dangled her feet in the water, wriggling her toes as it ran, cold and clean, up to her ankles. Beth showed Grace how to lay the dirty clothes out on the smooth rocks and rub them with soap. Grace rubbed until her arms ached.

Beth was easily out of breath, as if the baby inside her left no room for air. 'I always work hard when Tom is away,' she said as she scrubbed. 'It makes the time go faster.'

When all the clothes were clean, Grace and Beth loaded them back into the baskets for the long walk up to the house. The baskets were much heavier now that the clothes were wet. Beth put her hand on her lower back, and looked up the hill.

'I can come back down for the second lot, Beth,' said Grace.

'No need for that. I'll be fine. I might look as big as Moll but I can still walk!'

'But Master Tom said . . .'

Beth turned to Grace. 'Master Tom – why do you call him that?'

Grace looked at the ground, pulling at a long piece of grass.

'Grace, is that what Tom told you to call him?'

Grace tore up the piece of grass. 'Yes.'

'When did he ask you to do that?'

Grace's heart beat harder. 'He didn't tell you?'

'No, he didn't.'

Grace dropped the torn grass, noticing the

green stain it left on her fingers. She sighed. 'It was when he found me touching his horse. I know I shouldn't have done it, Beth. I know it was wrong – I only wanted to be close to Glory!' Grace bit her bottom lip. 'He found me with her and he was angry. That's when he told me to call him Master Tom.'

Beth sighed and sat down heavily on a large rock, resting her basket of wet clothes on her knees. 'Oh, Grace ...' She shook her head. 'There's so much you don't know about Tom.' Beth patted the rock beside her and Grace sat down next to her mistress, wondering what she meant. 'He had no family back in England. He was an orphan and a chimney sweep, until he got too big to fit up a chimney. Then his master threw him onto the streets. He was a common thief – like the rest of us.' Beth put her hand on Grace's knee. 'He never had anything to love. That's why that bleedin' horse is everything to him. He always wanted a horse of his own.'

Just like me, thought Grace.

'He wants to be Master Tom,' Beth went on, 'to be in charge and to leave the past behind – but I can't have you calling him that. Next he'll ask *me* to! Just call him Tom and I'll talk to him about it.' Beth looked up at Grace, shielding her eyes from the sun with her hand. 'You don't need to be so scared of him, Grace. He just takes a bit of time. And stay away from that flamin' horse of his. He's just silly about her.' Beth stuck out her arm. 'Now help me up so we can climb this stupid hill and make ourselves some lunch.'

Tom and me are not so very different, Grace thought as she got to her feet. Maybe that's why he always seems angry with me. Maybe I remind him of the things he wants to forget.

Grace remembered the chimney sweeps back in London, pushed up so many narrow chimneys by their masters that their bones never grew straight. As Grace walked back up the hill with her mistress, she thought about Wattle Park and the sheep and the cow and the chicken pen and the hut. Tom has done all this *and* he has a horse of his own. His life is very different to the way it was in London. Grace realised she wasn't so scared of Tom returning home now that she knew where he had come from.

For the next three days, Beth and Grace worked hard. They dug in the vegetable garden, pulled up weeds, cleaned the house, collected firewood and sewed by the fireside in the evenings. The only chore Beth didn't share with Grace was tending to Glory. Grace watched as Beth led the mare to different parts of the cleared green hillside and hobbled her so that she might feed on the fresh spring grass without straying.

After lunch the next day, Grace fetched the milking stool as Beth walk across the field carrying a bucket of maize towards the caramel-coloured cow.

'Come on, Moll, come on, girl, it's milking time,' she called. Moll stuck her nose in the bucket and followed Beth as she walked back to the fence where Grace stood. Next she attached a rope to Moll's halter and tied her to one of the fence palings with the bucket of feed on the ground in front of her. She tethered one of Moll's back legs to the fence, too.

'Does she like to be milked?' Grace asked, as Beth placed the milking stool close to Moll's swollen udder.

'Well, I'm not sure she likes it when I do it,' Beth answered. 'I'm not very good, even though Jerry showed me – did you know he grew up on a farm? He's the one who teaches me and Tom everything we need to know. But I never seem to get the hang of it.' Beth sat down on the stool. 'Come down here beside me and watch. See? You don't have to be afraid because her back leg is tied so she won't kick you – or the bucket – if you squeeze too hard.'

Grace crouched next to her. Cows smell a little like horses, she thought. Hay and warmth and grass.

Beth wrapped her hands around two of Moll's teats and squeezed. 'You pull from the top down, see, and if the milk won't come you give it a push with your hand, like this.' She knocked her hand up against Moll's udder. 'That's what the calves do with their muzzles if their mother's not letting down the milk.' A thin squirt of milk came shooting from one of the teats into the bucket. 'You pull one at a time, like this ... ' Beth pulled on Moll's teats. 'But when Jerry does it he gets three times the milk that I get.' Moll snorted as she chewed her dinner. 'You have a try, Grace.'

Beth heaved herself up so that Grace could sit on the stool. If only Hannah could see me now, Grace thought, milking a cow! She would probably try and squirt me with the milk! Grace leaned in against Moll and put her hands on the cow's teats. She pulled. Nothing came out.

'From the top down, remember. Like you're forcing the milk through with your fingers,' said Beth bending over to have a closer look.

Grace squeezed the teats from the top down and two long squirts of milk splashed into the bucket. Grace squealed. 'It worked!'

'Keep going, Grace. Keep going!'

Grace kept squeezing, resting her head against Moll's warm, wide stomach as she worked. Milk splashed against the tin sides of the bucket.

'She likes you, Grace. I think you might have found your true calling.'

'I think I have, Beth!' Grace kept milking and the two white streams entering the bucket became thicker and stronger. Beth leaned against the fence humming a soft tune, and Grace fell into a rhythm made up of Beth's song and the milk hitting the pail. *Squirtsquirt, squirtsquirt, squirtsquirt.*

Then Grace heard Beth moan beside her.

She turned to see Beth bend forward and clutch her belly. 'Beth, what is it? Are you all right?'

Beth moaned again.

'Are you sick?' Grace jumped to her feet, sending the bucket of new milk spilling across the ground.

'Oh, Grace . . . it feels like a knife in my stomach!' She fell to her knees on the milk-stained grass.

'Oh, Beth . . . ' Grace dropped down beside her mistress.

Beth dug her fingers into the earth and drew her breath in pain.

Grace looked at Beth's stomach, so round and hard and full. 'Beth, is it . . . could it be . . . ?' She put her hand gently on Beth's arm.

'No – no, the baby isn't due for weeks!'

Grace saw the fear in Beth's eyes. 'But, Beth – could it be?'

Beth was breathing hard. 'I don't know – I don't know – maybe I was wrong . . . or maybe it's early ... ' She gasped and gripped Grace's arm. Her face was white and there was a sheen of sweat across her brow. Her fingernails bit into Grace's skin. 'Oh, Grace!'

Grace felt her blood rush with fear. She didn't know anything about how to have a baby – she'd never had a brother or a sister – and they were so far from everyone.

She helped Beth to her feet.

'Grace, can you come with me into the house? Maybe if I lie down, the pain will stop.'

But Grace didn't think it was going to stop. Once Ma Honeywell's screaming and groaning started next door, there wasn't a break until the baby was born. As Grace helped her mistress into the hut, she could feel her trembling. I wish Liza were here, Grace thought. Liza would know what to do.

'Grace, can you – can you – make a bed for me here where you sleep – by the fire?' Beth panted between her words.

Grace unrolled her bedding and set it up for Beth, close to the hearth.

'If I lie down and rest, this blasted pain will go away and the baby can wait for its father to come home.'

'But Tom isn't back for two more days!'

'He'll be back in time! Please, Grace, make the fire warm.'

Grace pushed logs into the fire until the flames leapt high. Beth lay in the bed and groaned, her fists clenching above the blanket, then unclenching. Grace sat beside her mistress on the floor pressing a wet cloth to her forehead. Beth began to cry. Grace wished desperately that she could do something more to help her mistress. She felt useless.

After what seemed like a very long time Grace had to go outside. It was so hot in the hut – so filled with Beth's suffering and fear. Grace took in deep breaths of cool air. Was there someone who could help – somebody close enough? She tried to remember what Tom had said at the table the week before he left – something about a neighbour – a woman – not too far away. What was it? That she was capable and had experience nursing the sick? But Beth needed help *now* – it would take Grace a whole day to follow the East Trail to see if she could find her. It was no use!

Beth called to her from inside the hut. 'Grace? Grace, where are you? Are you there?'

'I'm coming, Beth, I'm just getting more wood for the fire!' In that instant, Glory whinnied, the sound carrying clearly from her field. Grace turned to go back inside. 'Neigh-eigh-eigh!' Glory whinnied again. It's as if she's calling me, Grace thought.

Glory called once more. 'Neigh-eigh-eigh!'

Grace gasped. An idea took hold. She ran into the hut.

Beth lay on her side with her eyes closed. Grace knelt beside her. 'Beth, ma'am, I'm here.' Beth's eyes remained closed. She's in another world, Grace thought, where there is nothing but pain.

Grace filled a mug with water from the kettle on the stove and brought it to her mistress. 'Can you drink, Beth?' But Beth did not respond. Grace saw dark patches of sweat forming under her arms and down the front of her chest. She placed the wet cloth on Beth's forehead.

'Beth, I have to go, but I will be back very soon.'

Beth opened her eyes and clutched Grace's arm. 'Please don't leave me, Grace, *please*!'

'But I must find help!'

'There is no one to help. If I just rest with you here to take care of me, everything will be all right.'

'No, Beth, the baby is coming. I have to go.'

Another wave of pain gripped Beth. She writhed and groaned.

'I'll be back soon, Beth, please hold on until then – please hold on.'

But Beth didn't answer. There was nothing more Grace could do for her at the hut; she had to leave – there was no time to waste.

## 9
### GRACE AND GLORY

GRACE rushed to the storage shed and grabbed Glory's bridle from its hook. Then she ran to the field behind the house. When the mare saw Grace, she lifted her head and pricked her ears.

Grace's heart raced. She pulled up a handful of grass and held it out to the mare. Glory ate the grass from Grace's open palm.

'Glory,' whispered Grace, running a hand across the horse's broad chest and looking into her eyes. 'Please help me.'

Glory pressed her nose into the crook of

Grace's arm and lowered her head. 'Thank you, Glory,' whispered Grace, lifting the bridle over the horse's ears just as she'd seen Tom do. She pressed the iron bit against Glory's mouth and pushed it in as she fitted the headpiece over the mare's ears.

Next she buckled the throat lash under the horse's cheek. Then, holding onto the reins, she bent down and unbuckled the hobbles from around Glory's fetlocks. She led the mare to the fence, looping the reins over her head.

Grace climbed to the second rung of the fence. Her legs were shaking and her chest felt as if it would burst.

'Glory, please look after me.' Grace grabbed onto Glory's mane with both hands and climbed onto her back. Glory shifted uneasily from side to side. Grace felt her own body stiffen. She ran her shaking hand down Glory's neck. *Please look after me.*

Grace pulled the right rein and Glory turned

her head and walked forward. 'We need to take the East Trail, down by the creek. Quickly Glory, we have to hurry.'

The mare began to jog and Grace jiggled awkwardly up and down on her back. She pulled hard on the reins, and Glory threw her head high in the air as if Grace had hurt her mouth.

'I'm sorry, Glory, I don't know how to do this!' Grace continued to jiggle and bounce as she steered Glory to the creek. The trail led both ways along the stream. Grace didn't know which direction to take – left or right.

Panic twisted in her stomach. What was I thinking? she wondered. I've left my mistress all alone to have a baby and I don't even know which way to go! Grace noticed that Glory was pulling her head towards the right. I wonder if Glory has carried Tom along this trail before? she thought. She decided that she had no choice but to trust the mare and go right.

'Hurry, Glory, hurry,' Grace clicked her tongue as she had heard the gentlemen riders do in London. Glory began to trot. Grace felt as though every part of her was being shaken and rattled by Glory's movements. Each time she came down on the horse's back she felt the breath being pushed out of her chest.

Suddenly Glory swerved to avoid a fallen log in the path and Grace lost her balance. '*Ahhh!*' She was thrown from the mare's back, landing on her face in the dirt. She sat up, wiping mud from her nose and mouth. 'Uch!' When she looked at her hand she saw a smear of blood across her fingers. Her nose was bleeding. Grace felt like giving up. Here she was sitting on her bottom in the mud and she didn't even know if she was going the right way.

Glory nibbled at the grass beside Grace's legs. Grace thought of Hannah. If Hannah were here, she would brush away the mud and the blood and ask that next time Grace fell, could she do a somersault on the way down please.

Glory pushed her head against Grace's shoulder. Grace stood up, gave her nose another wipe with her skirt and led the mare close to the fallen log. Climbing to its highest end and holding on to Glory's mane, she hauled her shaking body back on to the horse.

This time she gripped the reins even tighter than before, but Glory threw her head up and down even more wildly. Grace squeezed her legs against Glory's sides. 'Glory, please go as fast as you can!'

Glory broke into a canter. Grace slid stiffly up and down the mare's back, feeling that at any second she would fall again. She was so frightened she felt as if her blood had stopped flowing.

The horse threw her head so high and pulled so hard that the reins slipped through Grace's sweating hands and she had to hold onto the mane instead. As the reins hung slack against Glory's neck, Grace could see that the mare stopped throwing her head around and her gait grew steadier. Grace leaned forward and picked up the reins again, but this time she didn't pull them so tight.

She allowed her body to loosen and for the first time she was aware of the horse's warm flesh through her dress, alive and reassuring.

Grace felt calmer. She stopped sliding about so much and began to breathe. The mare's gait was as steady and rhythmical as a song. We are keeping the same time, Glory, Grace thought, as she moved with the horse. Even though Grace wished, with her whole heart, that Beth was not alone and suffering, as she cantered along the track in the afternoon light, Grace felt free.

The trail twisted and turned. Grace ducked her head from low-hanging branches, leaning down against Glory's shoulders. 'Faster, Glory, faster!' Grace leaned forward and the mare began to gallop. Grace could see Glory's legs thundering before her along the trail. She smelled horse and bush. Branches whipped at her face, a cold wind blew around her head and the sound of the mare's pounding hooves filled the air. Grace barely noticed the trees ripping and tearing at her dress, her trembling cold body or the steam rising from Glory's damp hide. She only knew she had to keep going, for Beth, for the baby.

The trail left the creek, turning uphill, before veering down again, pitted with stones and fallen branches. Many times Grace thought the track had ended, but then it would appear again, snaking through the dark, rough earth.

At last it opened out into a field. Grace could hardly believe her eyes when she saw a hut a little like Tom and Beth's, surrounded by cleared land. Smoke rose out of the hut's bark chimney. Smoke! Somebody was home — somebody who might be able to help.

Grace thought she might cry with relief.

Glory had chosen the best path and Grace had been right to trust her. The mare slowed to a walk as she approached the hut. Grace slipped from the horse, her legs buckling so that she fell in a heap to the ground. Glory snorted. A dog barked and strained at his rope. Grace tried to get up but her legs gave way again.

Then someone came out of the hut.

GRACE felt choked and when she tried to call out, her lips were too cold. Her face was frozen. She was shaking. She looked up and straight into the face of . . . Liza.

*Liza!*

'Grace!' Liza looked as shocked as Grace felt.

Grace opened her mouth to speak but no words came out.

'Grace? Is it you?'

Grace could only gape and nod.

Liza turned back to the hut. 'Hannah! It's Grace! Grace has come to us!' she called.

Grace wondered if she was dreaming.

Hannah ran out the front door of the house towards her. 'Grace! Grace!'

Grace struggled to speak, her words caught in her tears.

Hannah cried, too, falling to her knees and wrapping her arms around her friend. 'Grace! Grace!' The girls clung to each other.

After a moment, Liza gently took Grace's hands. 'Grace, dear girl, it's really you. Are you all right?' She touched Grace's bloodied cheek. 'What happened to you?'

'It's nothing. Please Liza ... Liza ...'

Liza turned to her daughter. 'Hannah, stop your crying. What is it, Grace?'

Grace gripped Liza's hands. 'My mistress is ... she's having a baby! Help me, Liza!'

Liza pulled her from the ground. 'Slow down, child – your mistress? Who is your mistress?'

'I – I – my mistress, Beth ... we don't live far

from here ... she's having a baby and I don't know what to do ... she's in terrible pain ... I'm afraid she might die!'

Hannah turned to her mother. 'The people who live along the East Trail, Mama! The Whitbys, isn't that what William said? Beth and Tom Whitby, and they've just chosen a servant – it must be our Grace!'

'Yes, yes, that's right,' said Grace, 'and Tom is away clearing land. The baby is coming early and Beth isn't ready!'

'Is someone with her now?' Liza asked.

Grace burst into tears all over again. 'No, she is all alone. I have left my mistress all alone!'

'Grace, calm down! I'll come and help her. Now tell me, Grace, this is very important – were there breaks between your mistress's pain, can you recall? Did she rest between the waves of pain?' asked Liza.

'Yes, I think so – I'm not sure – it was hurting her something awful!'

Liza turned to her daughter. 'Hannah, go and bring Grace something to eat and drink. Make sure you're quick about it. And give her your coat, too. I don't know how you made it all the way here on that bloomin' great horse without a saddle. You must be a natural, Grace.'

'Glory is a good horse. She did all the work.' Grace felt calmer now; she knew that Liza would take care of things.

Liza turned back to Grace. 'William, my new husband, is away working, too, so we'll have to do this alone. I'm going to put a saddle on Hilary, our workhorse, and one on yours, too, Grace, and then we will go. We'll have to hurry.' Liza looked up at the sky. 'It looks like rain is coming.'

HANNAH hugged Grace hard, her cheek, wet with tears, pressing against Grace's own. 'You are brave, Princess Grace,' she whispered as she helped her up onto the saddle on Glory's back. 'And a good rider, too. I don't know how you did it.'

'I did it because I had to,' Grace answered, pulling her friend's coat tightly around her shoulders.

'I'll see you again soon, Grace. Now that I know where you are, I will come and find you.' Glory began to move off. Hannah squeezed

Grace's hand.

'Come on, Grace.' Liza picked up the reins of her huge bay workhorse, turning her towards the track, her feathered hooves leaving deep impressions behind her in the mud. 'Your horse knows the way better than mine. I will follow. We must take care. Will said the spring rains can be very heavy.'

'Goodbye, Hannah!' Grace leaned forward and Glory broke into a canter. Grace gripped onto the rise at the front of the saddle and held on firmly with her legs. Glory knows we're heading for home, she thought.

Grace and Liza galloped along the track, the branches across the trail snatching at their arms and legs. It began to rain. Mud splattered up from beneath Glory's hooves, hitting Grace's cheeks and arms. She couldn't see ahead of her for the rain in her eyes. The trail seemed to go and on.

Finally it came to the creek and Grace

knew Wattle Park was not much further. She squeezed her legs harder against Glory. 'As fast as you can, girl!' Glory galloped even faster, with Hilary close behind, as if even the horses knew Beth was in danger.

At last the house came into view. Glory charged towards the fence then came to a sudden halt, sending Grace flying. She landed hard on her bottom beside Glory's front legs.

'Grace, are you all right?' Liza clambered down from Hilary, out of breath.

'Yes.' Grace pulled herself unsteadily to her feet. 'I didn't expect her to stop so suddenly!' As Grace turned to pat the mare, she saw a long gash down Glory's side, just below where the saddle had been. The cut was bleeding. Grace was horrified. Glory's sides heaved as the steam rose from her hide.

'There's no time to worry about her now,' said Liza. 'Quickly, Grace, unsaddle the horses and put them in the field, then come inside.'

Oh, Glory ... poor Glory ... Tom will never forgive me, Grace thought, as her numb, shaking fingers fumbled at the buckles on the saddles. That gash must have been made by a sharp branch on the trail. Grace felt sick with guilt and worry.

She ran, drenched, inside the hut. Beth lay as Grace had left her, eyes closed. When Grace saw her chest rising and falling with her breath, she was flooded with relief. 'Oh, Beth! Beth! I am back!' She ran to her mistress's side.

Liza was lighting the slush lamps. 'Quick, Grace, bring in wood and get the fire going nice and hot, and then boil some water. *Quick!* We need to get the hut ready before we're in darkness.' Liza took clean sheets and towels from the shelf and went over to Beth. She spoke to her calmly and softly, as though there was no danger and Beth was completely safe. Liza's comforting voice made Grace feel calmer, too.

'Everything will be fine now, Beth. My name is Liza and I'm here to help you have your baby.'

Beth opened her eyes wide and cried out as though a great wave of pain was bearing down on her. Grace put a large pot of water on the stove as Liza had told her.

Liza held Beth's hand until the pain passed. 'Grace, scrub your hands with soap and then come and sit by Beth's head. Beth, can you speak to me? Are you all right?'

Beth was panting. 'Yes – yes . . . is the baby coming?'

Liza put a hand gently to Beth's forehead. 'Yes, the baby's coming. We must work hard together to bring the baby out.'

Grace washed her hands and then came to Beth. Beth grabbed her arm.

'Oh, Grace, I thought you'd left me.'

'I'm sorry, Beth, but I had to get help.'

'And I'm glad – though I don't know how you did it.' She cried out in pain again, squeezing

Grace's hand so hard that Grace thought she might break it.

Liza laid out the towels and cloths under Beth and helped her to take off her dress and put her nightgown over her shoulders. Then she sat on the floor at the end of the bed. Grace stayed beside Beth's head, giving her sips of water and wiping the sweat from her brow.

'You must push now, Beth, push as hard as you can,' said Liza.

Beth clutched Grace's hand.

'Push!' Grace whispered. '*Push!*'

Grace was concentrating so hard on Beth that she was taken by surprise when Liza said, 'Yes, Beth! The baby is here!'

Liza lifted up the damp new baby and Beth began to cry as she took it into her arms. 'It's a girl,' said Liza. 'A beautiful baby girl. Well done, Beth.'

Beth held her baby against her chest and cried and laughed at the same time. Grace looked at the baby's tiny hands and feet, at the damp dark hair covering her head and her soft pink lips.

She's perfect, Grace thought. She noticed the way Beth looked down at her newborn, her face soft with love and tenderness.

Suddenly, Grace felt uncertain. Maybe now I will be on my own again, she worried.

As if sensing her feelings, Beth reached out and took Grace's hand. 'Oh, Grace, what would I have done without you? You were so brave.' Beth looked down at her baby. 'What do you think of the name *Alice*, Grace? Do you like it?'

'I like it very much,' Grace answered.

'Lovely little Alice.' Beth closed her eyes and held her new baby close.

Grace touched the soft new skin on Alice's arm and her heart felt as though it was pressing against the bones in her chest.

'I think it's time you had some rest, Beth.' Liza pulled the blankets up over her. 'Grace, your mistress will be very tired after all that work. Can you pour some warm water into the pail? Alice needs to be washed and swaddled and then she will need to rest, too.'

Liza and Grace set about making a cot for Alice. Grace found a wooden box in the shed and Liza took a pair of Tom's thick work trousers from off the line to make a mattress. Grace covered the trousers with newly hemmed tablecloths, then she placed the cot on the floor beside Beth's mattress.

'A bed for Alice,' said Grace.

Liza stayed the night with Beth and Grace, showing Beth how to feed her baby and how to take care of her. She told Beth that she must rest for the next few days, and only get out of bed to use the privy. Grace was to do everything – wash the nappies, bring meals for Beth, keep the hut warm and clean, bring firewood and prepare food as well as checking on the animals.

'It won't be for long, Grace. Tom will be home soon, and then he can take care of things.' Beth smiled weakly. 'Alice and I, we need you ...'

Grace didn't mind taking care of things. Beth had taught her so much. She could tend a garden, bake bread, feed chickens and wash clothes in a creek. Why, she could even milk a cow! Grace knew she was a good servant now, and it made her feel proud.

As Beth slept, Grace checked on Alice. She was wrapped in a faded yellow blanket in the makeshift cot. When Grace leaned over, the baby opened her deep blue eyes and looked at her. Grace reached out and touched her tiny hand. Immediately, Alice wrapped her fingers around Grace's thumb and held on.

'Hello, Alice,' Grace whispered. Alice gazed back at her. 'I'm going to do everything I can to help look after you.'

The next morning it was time for Liza to leave.

'I'm sorry I can't stay longer, but I must get back to Hannah, and then I have to be a midwife for three cows soon to calve,' she said, hugging Grace. 'Who would have thought that I would be bringing calves into the world as well as babies!' She set Grace back. 'And now that we've discovered how close we are, we'll be seeing each other again very soon. Hannah will be so happy – she was missing you something terrible. She was getting very lonely with only our sheep to tell her stories to!'

Grace held Liza tight one more time. She wished she knew when she would be seeing her friends again.

After Liza had left, Grace took a bucket of turnips and corn down to the field to give to Glory. She checked the mare's side – the blood had dried but the long jagged cut looked swollen and sore. Grace stroked Glory's face and the horse pushed her head against Grace's shoulder.

'I'm so sorry you got hurt, Glory. Tom will be very unhappy when he sees. But it's because of you that Beth is safe inside with her new baby,' she said. She buried her face in the horse's mane. 'Thank you, Glory.'

Then Grace sang a song she had learned on the streets of London:

*Lavender's green, diddle diddle*
*Lavender's blue,*
*You must love me, diddle diddle*
*Because I love you.*

When Grace lifted her head she heard the baby crying inside. Beth needs me, she thought. And so does Alice.

As she walked back up to the house, Grace felt the bright morning sun on her cheeks and she smiled.

# HOW I BECAME AN AUSTRALIAN GIRL

by Sofie Laguna

My father was born in Poland. When he was a small boy, war broke out in his country and he was placed in a camp with his mother and his little sister. After the war, my grandmother took him to Australia to begin a new life.

My mother was born in Holland. In Europe, Australia was seen as a country where anything was possible – a country of dreams. My grandparents brought my mother to live here when she was six.

My father met my mother when he was working as a doctor in a hospital in Sydney where my mother was a nurse. I was born in 1968 – their first Australian Girl.

I feel lucky to live in a peaceful country like Australia where I can make my dream of writing stories come true.

**HOW I BECAME AN AUSTRALIAN GIRL**

by Lucia Masciullo

I was born and grew up in Italy, a beautiful country to visit, but also a difficult country to live in for new generations.

In 2006, I packed up my suitcase and I left Italy with the man I love. We bet on Australia. I didn't know much about Australia before coming – I was just looking for new opportunities, I guess.

And I liked it right from the beginning! Australian people are resourceful, open-minded and always with a smile on their faces. I think all Australians keep in their blood a bit of the pioneer heritage, regardless of their own birthplace.

Here I began a new life and now I'm doing what I always dreamed of: I illustrate stories. Here is the place where I'd like to live and to grow up my children, in a country that doesn't fear the future.

**P**arramatta, the area where Grace goes to live with Beth and Tom, was founded in 1788, the same year that the First Fleet arrived in Sydney Cove. Governor Arthur Phillip decided that the soil in Sydney Cove was too sandy and poor to grow enough food for the new colony, so he chose Parramatta (which was originally called Rose Hill) as the best place for a large, successful farm.

The land around Parramatta was divided up and allotted to convicts once they had served their time. Tom, Grace's master, is an example of one of these convicts. He would have worked in the colony as a prisoner – building roads and houses, clearing land and pulling heavy loads – until finally finishing his sentence and being allotted land.

Life would have been very challenging for people from the busy city streets of London who knew nothing about farming in Australian conditions. They had to learn a lot in a short time, and work very hard if they were to survive.

Even building somewhere suitable to live was a challenge. New settlers had to build their huts from the materials they could find around them, like bark and mud and tree branches. Doors hung on leather hinges and window shutters were made of twigs.

The settlers who succeeded on the land had to be open to new ways of doing things, to experimentation, and to eating things they had never thought of as food before – like kangaroo and stinging nettles! Many freed prisoners lost their land through inexperience or bad planning, but if you were determined and you persevered, as Beth and Tom do, it was possible to make a new life that reaped many rewards.

Just like Grace, the early settlers found kangaroos fascinating. The native animals of Australia were so very different to those in Britain that they must have seemed like magical creatures. The name 'kangaroo' was first recorded by Captain Cook in 1770. It comes from the Guugu Yimithirr word *gangurru*. Guugu Yimithirr is the language of the Indigenous people who lived in north-east Queensland.

## DID YOU KNOW THESE THINGS ABOUT OUR CONVICT PAST?

The youngest convict on the First Fleet was James Grace and he was 11.

In 1790, a ship called the Lady Juliana transported 225 female convicts to Australia as part of the Second Fleet.

The British Government ended the transportation of convicts to Australia in 1868, by which time they had transported 162,000 convicts.

Before being transported, some convicts made 'convict love tokens', which were pennies they engraved with messages and left behind for friends and family, asking not to be forgotten.

While most convicts were from Britain or Ireland, there were also Maoris from New Zealand, Chinese from Hong Kong and slaves from the Caribbean.

One of the reasons Britain started sending convicts to Australia was because they couldn't send them to their colony in America anymore after America beat Britain in the American War of Independence.

Some Irish convicts were transported to Australia just for 'looking suspicious'!

Want to find out more?

Turn the page for a
sneak peek at Book 4

# A HOME
# FOR GRACE

'**G**RACE, would you put the kettle on for our hard-working men?' asked Beth from where she sat on her bed, cradling baby Alice as Jerry and Tom admired her. 'Anyone would think they'd just had a baby the way they carry on!' she said with a wink. Grace wished she felt as playful and happy as everyone else in the room but she could hardly manage a smile

'Tom,' Beth continued, 'did you know that if it weren't for our Grace you might have come home to a very different picture?'

She smiled at Grace. 'The baby started to come and we didn't know what to do, but Grace found help.'

'Help?' Tom frowned.

'She remembered our new neighbours, Tom, and she fetched Liza, the wife. Turns out they came out on the very same ship together from England! It was Liza who brought Alice safely into the world.'

'But how did Grace get all the way to the Clays' property? It's a fair distance along the East Trail. She must have walked the whole day . . .' Tom looked at Grace, his eyebrows raised.

Beth sat up higher in her bed. 'She took Glory. And Glory did you proud. She carried Grace all the way there and back.'

Grace stood back against the wall of the hut. The room felt very hot. Sweat dripped down the backs of her legs. Tom looked at her slowly. Ever since she had arrived at Wattle Park, Tom had treated her with suspicion. He had never trusted her around his precious horse, as if she might deliberately do something to hurt her. The way Tom was looking at her now made Grace feel ashamed, even though she knew she had never meant any harm or intended to do wrong.

Grace worried that if things didn't improve between them, Tom might send her back to the Factory. During her time there she had heard about convict-servants who had so disappointed their new masters that they had to be returned in exchange for better ones. Grace swallowed. She would rather die than be returned to the Factory – so far away from Hannah and Liza, and Beth and Alice – back where it was violent and dangerous. She felt her face grow hot under Tom's slow stare.

Beth placed her hand firmly on her

husband's arm. 'Aren't you going to thank Grace, Tom, for making sure our baby was born safe and that I was taken care of while you was away?'

The room was silent. Grace wished the wall would pull her straight through it and put her safely on the other side beside Jerry's tethered horse and wagon. How tempted she would be to ride away.

'Thank you, Grace,' Tom muttered, looking away.

But Grace knew Tom wouldn't want to thank her when he saw what had happened to his horse. How could he possibly let her stay at Wattle Park when he saw Glory's awful wound?

Grace . 1808

*Meet the other Australian girls and authors*

## LETTY ON THE LAND
### 1841

It's 1841 and if Letty wants to keep her job she must travel with her mistress to a sheep farm in the Blue Mountains, leaving her sister Lavinia behind in Sydney. Letty has heard that the bush is a wild place, full of strange beasts and dangers, not to mention the bushrangers that the local people are so afraid of. And as Letty soon learns, life on the land is full of all these things and more ...

Join Letty again on her adventure in the third of four exciting stories about a free-settler girl and her new life in a far-off land.

**Alison Lloyd**, author of the Letty books, is the popular and highly regarded author of several books for children, including *Year of the Tiger* and *Wicked Warriors and Evil Emperors*, a fantastic and fact-filled book about Ancient China.

## *Poppy and the Thief*
### *1864*

It's 1864 and Poppy is on the road again, heading to the town of Wahgunyah. On the way she meets a stranger who seems to know something about her past, and her special letter with the red tiger seal. But the more time she spends with this boy, the more difficult he becomes. Should Poppy trust him?

Join Poppy again on her adventure in the third of four stories about a Gold Rush girl who dreams of a better life.

**Gabrielle Wang**, author of the Poppy books, is a much loved writer for young people. Gabrielle's recent books include her bestselling Young Adult novel *Little Paradise,* and the very popular *Ghost in My Suitcase*, which won the 2009 Aurealis Award for young fiction.

## *Rose's Challenge*
### 1900

It's 1900 and Rose's world is changing. At last she can go to a proper school where she makes a best friend, learns more than just embroidery and even gets to play in a proper cricket match. But at home, Mother is dangerously ill, Father is worried about Federation, and Aunt Alice is getting in more trouble than ever ...

Join Rose again on her adventure in the third of four stories about a Federation girl who's determined to do things her way!

**Sherryl Clark**, author of the Rose books, is a prolific and popular writer for children. Sherryl's most recent Puffin book is *Motormouth*, a companion volume to *Sixth Grade Style Queen (Not!)*, which was an Honour Book in the 2008 CBC Book of the Year Award, Younger Readers.

Follow the story of your favourite
Australian girls and you will see that there
is a special charm on the cover of each book
that tells you something about the story.

Here they all are. You can tick them
off as you read each one.

**Meet Grace**

**A Friend
for Grace**

✓

**Grace
and Glory**

**A Home
for Grace**

**MEET LETTY**

**LETTY AND THE
STRANGER'S LACE**

**LETTY
ON THE LAND**

**LETTY'S
CHRISTMAS**

*Meet Poppy*

*Poppy at
Summerhill*

*Poppy and
the Thief*

*Poppy
Comes Home*

*Meet Rose*

*Rose on Wheels*

*Rose's
Challenge*

*Rose in Bloom*

**Meet Nellie**

**Nellie and the Letter**

**Nellie's Luck**

**Nellie's Greatest Wish**

**Meet Alice**

**Alice and the Apple Blossom Fair**

**Alice at Peppermint Grove**

**Peacetime for Alice**

**Meet Lina**

**Lina's Many Lives**

**Lina at the Games**

**A Lesson for Lina**

**Meet Ruby**

**Ruby and the Country Cousins**

**School Days for Ruby**

**Ruby of Kettle Farm**

**Meet Daisy**

**Daisy All Alone**

**Daisy in the Mansion**

**Daisy on the Road**

**Meet Pearlie**

**Pearlie's Pet Rescue**

**Pearlie the Spy**

**Pearlie's Ghost**

*A girl like me in a time gone by*

# WHICH AUSTRALIAN GIRL
# ARE YOU MOST LIKE?

To find out, read the questions below. On a piece of paper, write down the letter that appears next to each answer you choose.

1  Which hobby do you like best?

Photography  H        Cricket  C
Horseriding  B        Reading  F
Singing  A            Ballet  E
Writing  G            Fashion  D

2  When things aren't going your way, are you most likely to . . .

Lose your temper and then regret it  F
Cry and hide yourself away for a while  D
Get cross and maybe even yell a little  C, G
Try your hardest to fix things  E
Distract yourself with your fave things  B, H
Make a plan to make things better  A

3  How would your friends describe you?

Dedicated and loyal  A
Light-hearted and life of the party  H
Always sunny and optimistic  F
Fun and outgoing, with lots of interests and hobbies  C
Once you trust people, you're friends for life  B
A bit of a perfectionist  E
Passionate and full of imagination  G
Sweet, generous and kind  D

4 **What would you like to be when you grow up?**
   A vet   B
   A diplomat   A
   A dancer   E
   A photographer   H
   A dress designer   D
   A journalist   G
   A teacher   C/F

5 **How would you most like to celebrate your birthday?**
   Have a fancy-dress party   H
   Curl up with your new book somewhere cosy   G
   Go to the beach with everyone you love   E
   Eat an enormous feast of all your favourite foods   F
   Have a big party with everyone you know   A
   Have your favourite food at home with your family   B
   Invite your six best friends over for a craft sleepover   D
   Have a picnic outside in a beautiful park   C

6 **Which book would you be most likely to read?**
   A book about mythical creatures in a fantasy land   F
   *The Secret Garden*   D
   *Black Beauty*   B
   *Diary of Anne Frank*   G
   A big book of interesting facts   A
   *Seven Little Australians*   E
   *Treasure Island*   C
   Nothing too serious   H

7 **How do you get on with your siblings?**

Sometimes we get on but sometimes they're really
annoying.　**C, G**

I look up to them, but sometimes I feel a bit left out.　**D**

I love playing games and hanging out with them.　**A**

They're my favourite person in the world.　**E**

I'm an only child.　**B, H**

I no longer live with them.　**F**

## RESULTS!
Look at the letters you've written down and
count up how many of each one you have.

### If you answered mostly As:
You are most similar to Poppy! Like Poppy, you're outgoing
and adventurous, and you love a new challenge. You're
popular and loyal, and you love getting together with
friends in the great outdoors.

### If you answered mostly Bs:
You and Grace have a lot in common – you're both dreamy
and quiet, and you can be a little shy at first. You love animals and
nature. Your imagination can get you through anything!

### If you answered mostly Cs:
You're a regular Rose – a determined girl who knows what
she wants. You have big dreams of travelling the world. You're
not afraid of standing up for yourself, and sometimes that can
lead to arguments! But underneath you have a heart of gold.

### If you answered mostly Ds:
You're just like Letty! Sometimes it can take you a while to
get used to new things, but that's okay! You're artistic, and
like sewing and craft. Watch out for people who might take
advantage of your kind and generous nature.

### If you answered mostly Es:

You're an Alice, for sure! You throw yourself into whatever you do, and you like to be good at it – maybe even the best. You're passionate and dedicated, but make sure you're not too hard on yourself! Nobody can be perfect all the time.

### If you answered mostly Fs:

You're most like Nellie – a people person with a big heart. But if you lose your temper – watch out! Keeping your cool could be your biggest challenge in life. You enjoy planning for the future, and might end up in a job where you can help other people. Bonus!

### If you answered mostly Gs:

You're a little Lina – creative, loyal, and full of imagination. If you can stay focused on the things that matter, you have the potential to go far. People love the way you fight for what you believe in. Remember to always be yourself – it's the most important thing.

### If you answered mostly Hs:

Ruby is the OAG you're most similar to – a chatty, dreamy girl who can't always sit still! You're always fun to be around and have a lot of things on the go, but try to make time to think about other people and be a good listener whenever you can.

### If you had a mixture of answers:

You're a little bit like all our OAGs! A bit dreamy, a bit sporty, sometimes shy and sometimes outgoing. You have lots of different friends and interests, and sometimes it might seem like you don't know what to do when you grow up. But don't worry – with talents like yours, there's heaps of time to decide.

For another quiz and heaps more fun activities, go to ouraustraliangirl.com.au.